ALBERT HOPPER,

SCIENCE HERO

WORMING TO THE CENTER OF THE EARTH!

John Himmelman

Henry Holt and Company
New York

For Alice.
There's just so much to see!

Henry Holt and Company, *Publishers since 1866*
Henry Holt® is a registered trademark of Macmillan Publishing Group, LLC
120 Broadway, New York, NY 10271 · mackids.com

Copyright © 2020 by John Himmelman

Library of Congress Control Number: 2019949149
ISBN 9781250230164

Our books may be purchased in bulk for promotional, educational, or business use.
Please contact your local bookseller or the Macmillan Corporate
and Premium Sales Department at (800) 221-7945 ext. 5442 or by email at
MacmillanSpecialMarkets@macmillan.com.

First edition, 2020 / Designed by Cindy De la Cruz
Printed in China by RR Donnelley Asia Printing Solutions Ltd.,
Dongguan City, Guangdong Province

1 3 5 7 9 10 8 6 4 2

CONTENTS

Worming to the Center of the Earth!

Professor Albert Hopper
is a Science Hero.

His heroic science mission?

EXPLORE THE WORLD AND BEYOND!

He is often joined by his two Junior Science Heroes, niece Polly and nephew Tad.

Come with them on their latest adventure . . .

WORMING TO THE CENTER OF THE EARTH!

Chapter 1
WIGGLES

"Calling Junior Science Hero Polly. Calling Junior Science Hero Tad. Report to the laboritorium, and quickly!"

Polly and Tad raced to their uncle's
lab. A huge metal worm filled the room.
"Behold! Our newest ship! I call it . . .
'Wiggles,'" said the Science Hero.

"We shall be . . . WORMING TO the CENTER OF THE EARTH! Come inside."

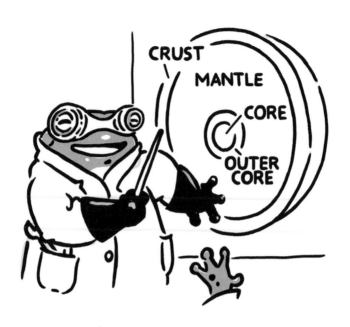

The scientist pulled out a chart.

"The Earth is a ball made of layers.
We will first drill through the *crust*.
It is mostly rocks and sand. Oh, and
tunnels of sizzling melted rock."

"Tunnels of *sizzling melted rock*?"
asked Tad.

"Yes," said his uncle.

"Then we will squeeze through the *mantle*. It will get more solid as we go deeper. If all goes well, we will reach the *outer core*."

"If all goes well?" asked Tad.

"Yes," said his uncle.

"The outer core will be a soupy burning magnet. Our engines may not work."

"We might get stuck?" asked Tad.

"Yes," said his uncle.

"From there, we land on the *inner core.*

"It is solid metal and hotter than the sun. It might melt our ship, but it might not."

"But it might?" asked Tad.

"Yes," said his uncle.

"Why are we doing this?" asked Tad.

"Knowledge and adventure!" shouted Polly.

"Precisely!" said their uncle.

"We shall be the very first to explore the inside of this planet! Who is coming aboard?"

"Junior Science Hero Polly reporting for duty," said his niece.

"Did our mom say it is okay?" asked Tad.

"Yes," said his uncle.

"And school said it is okay?"

"Yes," said his uncle.

"Okay," said Tad.

"Junior Science Hero Tad, blah blah blah . . ."

"When do we go?" asked Polly.

"At this VERY moment!" said the hero of science.

He yanked some levers.

He twisted some knobs.

The ship came alive!

It rammed its nose into the floor

and began to dig.

"Do you remember the rule about the A-C-H button?" asked the professor.

"Never, ever press the 'Anything Can Happen' button," recited Polly and Tad.

"Correct!" said their uncle.

"Then why did you add it?" asked Polly.

"Just in case," said her uncle.

"I am pressing it," said Tad.

"Do NOT!" said his uncle.

Tad's finger inched toward the button.

"It's a button," he said.

"I have to press it."

"Don't do it, Tad," said Polly.

Tad's finger touched the button.

"I cannot NOT press it!" shouted Tad.

"You must not NOT press it!"
ordered his uncle.

"YOU JUST TOLD HIM TO PRESS IT!"
cried Polly.

Tad pressed the button.

"Sorry," he said.

"What happens now?" asked Polly, as they tunneled into the Earth's crust.

The Science Hero sighed.

"Anything."

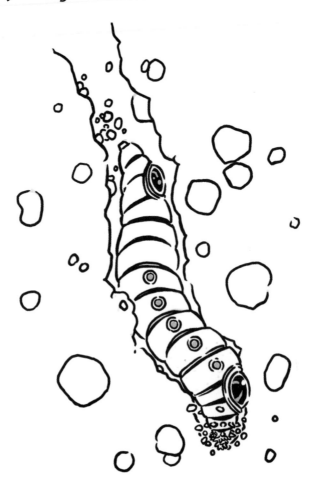

Chapter 2
CAVERN OF THE CAVEFROGS

The ship squirmed through the crust.

"What's that crunchy-crunchy noise?" asked Tad.

"Wiggles is eating the rocks," said the Science Hero.

"Where do they go?" asked his nephew.

Albert Hopper patted a tube that ran through the ship.

"They go through here and out the other end," he said.

"It's like an earthworm," said Polly.

"That was my very inspiration, my brilliant niece."

Polly looked at the controls. "We are a mile deep already!"

Suddenly, the crunching stopped.

The ship dropped into a large cavern.

"It seems that our first mission has found us," said the professor.

"We shall explore this . . . UNEXPLORED CAVERN!

Install your light helmets!"

"*Install?*" asked Tad.

"Put it on your head," said Polly.

They entered the cavern.

"Set your lights at their brightest setting," warned the professor.

"It's darker than dark in here."

"Ow!" said Tad.

"Are you okay?" asked his uncle.

"It was just my head," said his nephew.

"I bumped into a *stalagmite*."

"If it's hanging from the ceiling it's a *stalacTITE*," said Polly.

"Oof!" said Tad.

"Have you sustained injury?" asked his uncle.

"Just my ears," said his nephew.
"They're tired of Polly's science facts.
Ooch!"

"Are you wounded?" asked his uncle.

"My head again," said his nephew.
"Polly hit me with a stalacTITE."

"Oooo, aim your beams on this!"
said the Science Hero.

They shone their lights on the wall.
It was covered with paintings.
"These have to be 10,000 years old!"
"Who made them?" asked Tad.
"Prehistoric cavefrogs," said Polly.
"But how did they get down here?"
"There might have been another
way in," said their uncle.

"They built fires so they could se=e,
and used the ashes as paint," he added.

The three studied the images.

"I'm copying the drawings," said Tad.

"Brilliant, my nephew!" said the professor.

"Oompa," echoed a voice from the darkness.

"What is—" began Polly.

"CAVEFROGS!" shouted Tad.

"RUN!" croaked their uncle.

The cavefrogs chased them through the dark tunnels.

"This is impossible!" said Albert Hopper. "Cavefrogs have been gone for thousands of years!"

"Unless," said Polly.

"Unless what?" asked her uncle.

Polly looked at her brother.

"Unless someone pressed an A-C-H button."

"I think they are following our lights," said Tad. "Turn them off!"

They turned off their headlamps.

"It sure is dark," said Polly.

"I think they're gone," said Tad.

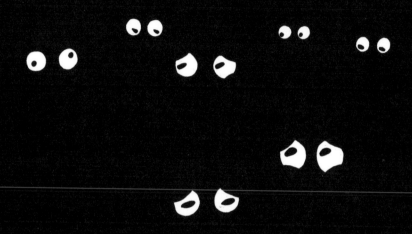

They turned their lights back on.

They were surrounded by the
cavefrogs!

"Oompa," said one of them.

The Science Hero held up his hands. "We come in peace," he said.

"Us, too," said the cavefrog. "My name is Oompa. This is Poompa. This is Roompa. This one's Terry . . ."

Oompa introduced the rest of the group.

"Just saying hi," he finished. "Have fun in your big worm."

The scientists returned to their ship.

"That was just . . . strange," said Polly.

"More strangeness awaits," said
Albert Hopper.

"As we press on with our journey
to . . . THE CENTER OF THE EARTH!"

Chapter 3

TEETH AND HORNS!

Wiggles twisted into the Earth.

"The crust here is about 30 miles thick," said the professor.

"Thirty miles thick of *what*?" asked Tad.

"Three kinds of rocks," said his uncle.

"*Sedimentary*, made from mud. *Igneous*, made from heat. And *metamorphic*, made from pressure."

"What's the one that looks like a
Tyrannosaurus rex?" asked Tad.

"A *fossil*," said Polly.

"Fossils are rocks that were once
bones."

"Okay," said Tad.

"And should it be chewing on
our ship?"

They ran to a window.

A *Tyrannosaurus* fossil was chomping on Wiggles.

"Someone should not have pressed a button he should not have pressed," said Polly.

Their uncle pulled a lever.

Wiggles spun faster, cracking through the rocky crust.

The toothy fossil held on tightly.

Then the ship stopped.

It was stuck in the horns of a *Triceratops.*

"It seems we are trapped in the *Cretaceous* period," said the professor.

"These fossils are about 68 million years old."

"I have an idea," said Polly.

"If we push through deeper, the fossils will get smaller."

"But we're stuck!" said Tad.

"Not for long," said the Science Hero.

"I'm setting the controls to . . . FULL WIGGLE!"

The ship twisted, jiggled, and shook.

Its crew was tossed about inside.

They broke free of the *Tyrannosaurus* and *Triceratops* . . . and slammed into a *Brachiosaurus*!

"They're getting even bigger!"
said Tad.

"You said they would get smaller!"

"Um . . . soon," said Polly.

"We must be in the *Jurassic* period.
That's about 154 million years deep."

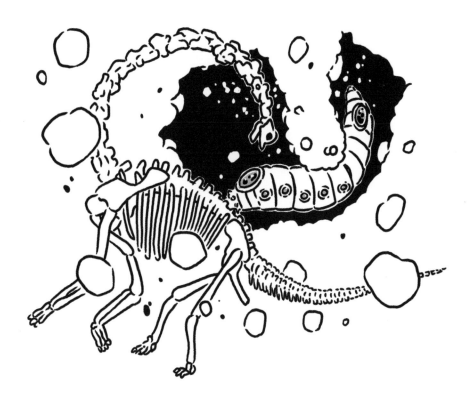

"Full Wiggle ahead!" shouted their uncle.

The ship squeezed past a *Diplodocus*.
It noodled by a pod of *Bobosaurus*.

"We're in the *Triassic* now," said the
professor.

"Two hundred twenty-eight million
years back," said Polly.

"Stop showing off!" shouted Tad.

The Science Hero pulled back on
the lever.

"DIG, I SAY! DIG!"

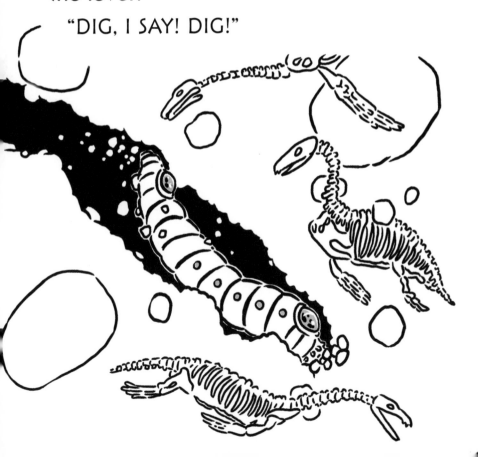

They crashed past *Dimetrodons.*

"*Permian* period," whispered Polly.

They weaseled by some trilobites.

"*Cambrian* period," whispered
her uncle.

"They're getting smaller," said Tad.

Soon the fossils were mostly fish.

"We're safe," said the Science Hero.

"And now, we continue our journey to—"

"Wait a minute," said Tad.

Wiggles stopped.

Tad crawled out the ship's hatch.

He returned with a fossil.

"For show-and-tell," he said.

Chapter 4
UH-OH

"Are we there yet?" asked Tad.

"We're barely through the crust, right, Uncle?" said Polly.

"Correct, Junior Science Hero Polly. We are scraping beneath the ocean through the . . . *OCEANIC PLATE!*"

"We're on a dish?" asked Tad.

"*Plate*, Junior Science Hero, oceanic *plate.*

"Plates are slabs of crust that move beneath our seas and continents.
"Hold steady on those controls, Polly. You must not puncture the seafloor from below."

"Got it," said Polly.

"A fish just swam past my window," said Tad.

"Doubtful!" said Albert Hopper.

"Uh-oh," said Polly. "I see fish, too."

"Doubtful!" said Albert Hopper,

"Unless . . . Uh-oh."

"That's two uh-ohs," said Tad.

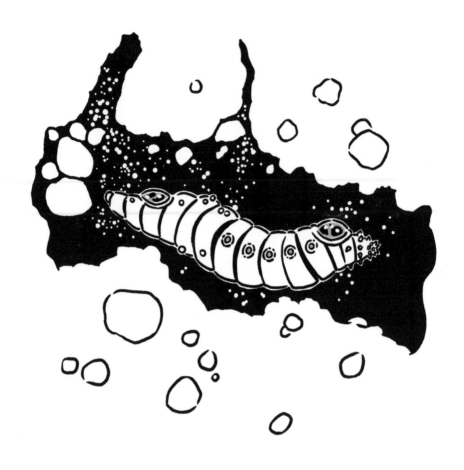

"Double those uh-ohs," said his uncle.
"The colossal pressure from the sea
has collapsed the tunnel behind us!
We're *blurping* through water!"

"What now?" cried Polly.

"It's starting to rain in here!" shouted Tad.

"Panic, everyone!" shrieked
their uncle.

"We're on it!" yelled Polly and Tad.

The heroes of science shrieked and
squealed as the sea chased them
through the oceanic dish!

"*Plate*," whispered the professor.

"Okay," he said. "Panic time over. Good job, all."

"The water is getting high in here," said Tad.

"This ship was not made for water," said his uncle.

"It's coming from behind us," said Polly.

"The more we dig, the more the tunnel fills with seawater."

"ACTIVATE THE PUMPS!" ordered her uncle.

"Pumps activated," said Polly.

The water was sucked out of the ship.

"Wait," she said. "What's that red stripe on the screen?"

"*Magma!*" said her uncle.

"We're in luck! Aim for it, young Polly! Aim for it with everything you've got!"

"What is magma?" asked Tad.

"Hot melted rock," said Polly.

"Over a . . . THOUSAND DEGREES!" said science's greatest hero.

"And we're aiming for it?" asked Tad.

"INTO THE MAGMA!" ordered his uncle.

The ship turned down and entered
the tunnel of magma.

With a mighty hiss, it squeezed into
the glowing orange tube.

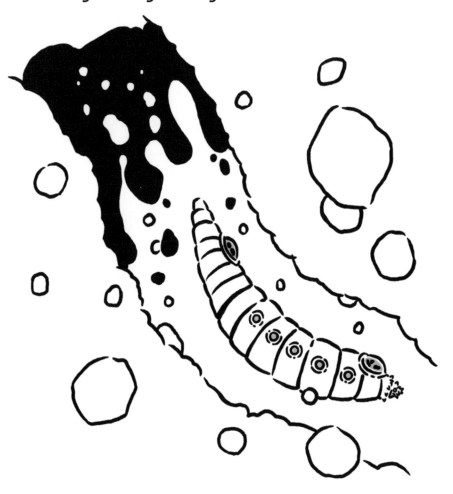

"Oh, I see," said Polly.

"Magma is thicker than water. It will hold it back."

"Precisely," said the professor.

"This ship is not waterproof, but it's pretty good in the heat."

"So we're floating in melted rocks?" asked Tad.

"Unquestionably," said his uncle.

"And on purpose?"

"Indubitably," said his uncle.

"We shall enter the burning magma as we continue our journey to . . . THE VERY CENTER OF THE EARTH!"

Chapter 5

DON'T TOUCH THE SIDES!

The Science Heroes slipped through an endless maze of magma tubes.

"How do we know where we're going?" asked Polly.

"We do not," said her uncle.

"It's like a maze," said Tad.

"Ouch, the ship's walls are hot."

"Didn't you read the chapter title?" asked his sister.

"Fear not," said Albert Hopper.
"The advanced technology of this ship will soon counter the heat. Junior Science Hero Polly?"

"Yep?"

"Engage the . . . AIR CONDITIONER!"

She flipped a switch.

The air conditioner clunked on.

"Ahhhh . . . ," said her uncle.

"Refreshing . . ."

One magma tunnel led to another.
They wriggled back and forth.
They squiggled up and down.
They wombled in every direction,
but there was no way out.

"Whenever you are in a maze," said Tad, "you go left three times and right one time."

"No you don't," said Polly.

"You touch one wall of the maze and keep your hand on it until you are out."

"Well, we can't do that," said her brother.

"See that hole in the ship's wall?" asked the professor.

"Shove your hand in it."

"There is NO way I am putting my hand in that hole!" said Tad.

"Oh, it's just a big metal glove, Tad," said his uncle.

"I won't burn my hand off?"

"Highly unlikely," assured the hero of science.

"Why don't *you* do it?" asked Tad.

"I must continue with my calculations," said the hero of excuses.

Tad started to slip his hand into the glove.

He pulled it back out.

"What if a spider crawled in it?"

"No spiders," said his uncle.

Tad slipped his hand inside.

"Good job, Tad. Now keep your hand on the tunnel's wall."

"This could take a while," said Polly.

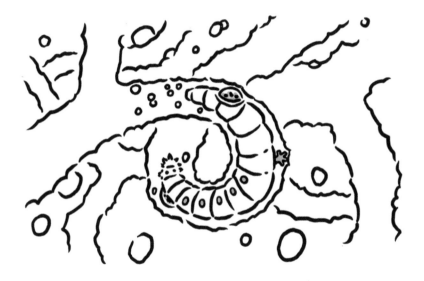

The crew felt their way through the tangle of tubes.

"Look on the screen!" said Polly.

"The tunnels lead to that big red blob!"

"The *magma chamber*!" said the professor. "All the molten rock collects there!"

"My arm is getting tired," said Tad.

"Extract it from the gauntlet, my nephew. Your work is done."

"Huh?"

"Pull it out of the glove," said Polly. They entered the magma chamber. The professor looked at the screen.

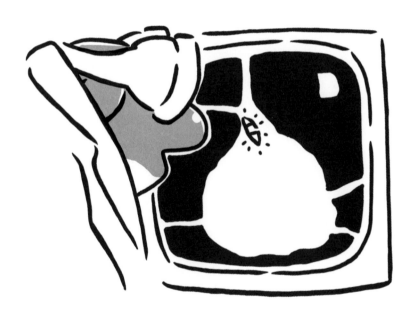

"Uh-oh," he said.

"Is that what I think it is?"

"It looks like a giant cone," said Tad, "with a red stripe going up the middle."

"Uh-oh," said Polly.

"And at the bottom of the red stripe," continued Tad, "is a big red blob."

"The magma chamber," said his uncle.

"What's that blinking thing in the middle?" asked Tad.

"Our ship," said Polly. "We're in a . . ."

"VOLCANO!" they all shouted.

The magma shot up the tube and carried them with it.

The ship burst through the cone.

"WHOOOOOAAAAA!" screamed the crew.

They were launched above the clouds and landed on top of the volcano.

Wiggles slid down the side.

"The magma is pulling us back down," said Tad.

"*Lava*," said Polly.

"It's called lava when it's outside of the volcano."

"That was very useful information, Polly," said Tad. "It solved all of our problems."

"Look," said their uncle, "a *vent*! That hole in the side of the volcano will lead back to the magma chamber.

"From there, we can tunnel straight down."

They steered Wiggles down the vent and made it back to the chamber.

"Take her down, Junior Science Hero Polly! We shall continue our mission to—"

"Wait," said Tad. "One more time?"

Albert Hopper smiled and turned to his niece.

"Junior Science Hero Polly?"

Polly smiled.

Chapter 6
SHAKY PLATES!

"Are we there yet?" asked Tad.

"We are still in the *lithosphere*," said his uncle.

"Polly, are you going to tell everyone what the lithosphere is?" asked her brother.

"Not if you don't want me to," she said.

"Are you sure? I know you want to."

"That's okay," said his sister.

"Good. Then the lithosphere—" began Tad.

"—is the layer between the lower crust and upper mantle," recited his sister.

"It is made up of big hunks of solid rock called *tectonic plates.*

"They move around across the crust
and make up the continents."

"Feel better?" asked Tad.

"Yes," said Polly.

The hero of science looked at his
niece and nephew.

"Stop jumping around," he said.

"We're not," said Polly. "*You* are."

"Hmm," said their uncle. "I may have some disturbing news. We seem to be experiencing an—"

The ship began to shake violently.

"EARTHQUAKE!" they all shouted.

"Find something . . . to hold on to!" ordered the professor.

"We . . . must . . . be . . . where . . . two . . . plates . . . are . . . rubbing . . . together!" said Polly.

"You . . . just . . . can't . . . help . . . your . . . self . . . can . . . you?" said her brother.

"If . . . this . . . keeps . . . up, Wiggles . . . will . . . fall . . . apart!" said their uncle. "Polly . . . try . . . to . . . steer . . . straight . . . down!"

"I . . . can't!" said Polly. "The . . . controls . . . shook . . . apart! They . . . are . . . flying . . . all . . . over . . . the . . . ship!"

"I . . . got . . . them!" shouted Tad.

"Put . . . them . . . back . . . together!" said science's shakiest hero.

"Really?" asked his niece.

"You . . . must," said her uncle, "before . . . the . . . ship . . . falls . . . to . . . pieces!"

"Tape! I need tape!" Polly shouted.

"Here," said Tad.

"Rubber bands! I need rubber bands!"

"Here," said Tad.

"They're . . . back . . . together . . . ,"
she said.

"Steer . . . the . . . ship . . . straight . . .
down," said her uncle.

"Hold . . . together . . . Wiggles!"

The ship spun and pounded through the lithosphere.

The heroes of science bounced around inside it.

Then the shaking stopped.

"You did it!" said Tad.

"Yes," said Albert Hopper.

"That was a scary one. But just a shaky bump in the mission, as we continue our journey to the . . . VERY CENTER OF—"

"I think we're stuck," said Polly.

"Drat," said her uncle.

Chapter 7
PASS THE CRATONS

"Junior Science Hero Polly. Junior Science Hero Tad. I have some unpleasant news for the both of you."

"I know. We're stuck," said Tad. "Polly said so in the last chapter."

"I thought Wiggles could tunnel through anything," said Polly.

"It appears we are in a *craton*," said their uncle.

They both looked to Polly.

She shrugged her shoulders.

"I don't know what that is," she said.

"Cratons," said her uncle, "are deep piles of very old rocks. This one goes all the way down into the upper mantle of the Earth!"

CRATONS

"We can't worm through it?" asked Tad.

"Negative," said his uncle.

"Look out the windows."

The Junior Science Heroes gasped.

"DIAMONDS!" they shouted.

"Precisely," said their uncle.

"One of the hardest elements known to frogkind. The deep cratons of Earth hold a QUADRILLION TONS of them."

"Wait a second," said Tad.

He pulled out his sketchpad.

"Is this a quadrillion?"

"For certain, young Tad," said his uncle.

"It is a ... THOUSAND BILLION!"

"A million trillion," said Polly.

"A hundred TEN TRILLION," said the professor.

"We're rich!" said Tad.

"No, we're stuck," said Polly.

"REVERSE ENGINES!" ordered their uncle.

They tried to back up the ship.

It didn't budge.

"RE-REVERSE ENGINES!" ordered their uncle.

Wiggles didn't move.

"The spinning nose is being stopped by the diamonds," said Polly. "It can't cut through them."

"Can it cut through the rock that is holding them?" asked Tad.

"Yes," said his uncle, "but the nose is too wide."

"Hammer drills!" said Polly.

"Yes, hammer drills!" said her uncle.

"Polly, you are a genius! Junior Science Heroes, suit up and fetch the hammer drills! We shall exit the ship to break up the very rock that traps the diamonds!"

"That could take years," said Polly.

"That is of little doubt," said her uncle.

They put on their upper mantle suits, grabbed the drills, and left the ship.

"Zip your suits up tightly," said the professor.

"At this depth, the mantle is over . . . **1,000 DEGREES!**"

They began drilling the rock between the diamonds.

"We could be doing this for the rest of our lives," said Polly.

"Perhaps longer," said her uncle.

"Through," said Tad.

"What?" asked his uncle.

"Through. I broke through," said his nephew.

"How could you—" began Polly.

"Look," Tad said.

"We must have been on the outer edge of the craton," said his sister.

"Well done, Junior Science Hero Tad," said his uncle.

The Science Heroes returned to Wiggles.

Tad's pockets were bulging.

"Those wouldn't be diamonds, would they?" asked his uncle.

Tad pointed to Polly.

"Ask her what is in *her* pockets," said her brother.

"Polly—" began her uncle, whose pockets were also bulging.

"Uncle, what is in your—" began his niece.

"Strap in, Junior Science Heroes," he interrupted, "As we guide this ship to . . . THE CENTER OF THE VERY EARTH ITSELF!"

Chapter 8
AUTOPILOT

"Are we there yet?" asked Tad.

"Not even close," said his uncle.

"We are in the mantle, and will be for some time. It is nearly 2,000 miles thick."

"How long before we reach the core?" asked Polly.

"A few weeks," said her uncle.

"Or months. Years, maybe.

"The mantle gets more solid as we go deeper. And hotter—up to 7,000 DEGREES! I suggest we let Wiggles's *autopilot* take over."

"Do you really trust that computer to steer the ship?" asked Polly.

"I think so," said her uncle. "Autopilot, take us through the mantle!"

IS THAT UP OR DOWN? asked the autopilot.

"Down!" said the Science Hero.

OKAY, OKAY . . . DOWN IT IS!

The ship tunneled through the mantle.

The three passengers found ways to pass the time.

Science Hero Albert Hopper did science-y things.

Junior Science Hero Polly read
through her library.

Tad watched TV.

UM, QUESTION, said the autopilot.

I HIT A HARD SPOT. SHOULD I GO AROUND IT, OR . . . TRY TO BREAK THROUGH?

"Around!" said Albert Hopper. "Go around, I say!"

A few hours later,

ER, QUESTION, said the autopilot.
*ANOTHER HARD SPOT AHEAD. GO
AROUND OR . . . BUST THROUGH?*

"Around! Around!" said the Science
Hero.

"Now please stop interrupting my science-y things."

OKAAAY, IF YOU SAY SO, sang the autopilot.

"I don't like the way it said that," said Tad.

Days passed.

The ship tunneled through the Earth.

Science Hero Albert Hopper did more science-y things.

Junior Science Hero Polly read
through her library, again.

Tad watched TV.

A few days later, the ship stopped.

WE'RE HEEERE, sang the autopilot.

"So soon?" asked the professor.

The ship began to shake.

Something pounded on it from outside.

"Uncle?" asked Polly. "Do they have *yetis* at the Earth's core?"

"Yetis?" asked Tad.

"Abominable snowmen," said his sister.

"First," said her uncle, "*abominable* is a big word for this reading level. And second, no."

"I think the autopilot got lost," said his niece.

"According to the readings we are 5.49 miles *above* the Earth!"

HAD TO KEEP GOING AROUND HARD SPOTS, said the autopilot.

LIKE YOU TOLD ME TO, it continued.

NOT MY FAULT, it finished.

"You have steered us to the very tippity top of the planet!" said the professor.

"And brought us to . . ."

"MOUNT EVEREST!" cried the Science Heroes.

"That would explain the yeti," said his niece.

"I didn't think they were real."

The professor pointed to the A-C-H button.

"*They might not have been,*" he muttered.

"What do we do about them?" asked Tad.

"Ignore them. They can't harm the ship," said his uncle.

"But one's making faces at me,"
said Tad.

"Then make faces back at it," said
his uncle.

"Junior Science Hero Polly? Take
over the controls!"

I CAN DO IT! said the autopilot.

"Nevertheless," said the professor. "Polly, steer straight down and don't stop until we hit ... THE OUTER CORE!"

AND GO AROUND THE HARD SPOTS, whispered the autopilot.

"Negative!" declared Albert Hopper.
"Smash through EVERYTHING until
we reach . . . THE VERY CENTER OF
THE EARTH!"

Chapter 9
THINGS STUCK TO THINGS

"Are we—" began Tad.

"No," said Polly.

"But almost!" said their uncle.

"We have reached the outer core!"

Wiggles sloshed through like a worm in mud.

"We are going through 1,500 miles of a thick liquid goo made of melted nickel and iron."

"The controls say it's 6,000 degrees out there," said Polly, "and getting hotter as we go deeper."

"Good that we're staying inside," said Tad.

"Of course," said his uncle.

"But only after we go outside. It will be a good test of our outer core exploration suits!"

"That's not called 'staying inside,'"
said his nephew.

Suddenly science's most adventurous
hero was pulled to the top of the
ship.

"I was afraid of this," he said.

"Uncle?" asked Polly.

"Yes?" answered the professor.

"Do you have something metal in
your pocket?" she asked.

"Why, yes, young Science Hero.
Yes, I do have something metal in my
pocket. My pen. And it's sticking to
the metal ceiling of the ship."

"This is where the Earth's *magnetic
force* comes from," said Polly to her
brother. "And—Tad?"

"Up here," said her brother.

He was stuck to the ceiling next to his uncle.

"Pen in your pocket, young nephew?" asked the professor.

"Spoon from lunch," he answered.

"We are in a strong magnetic force field," said his uncle.

"We need to find our way to an area where it is weaker."

"I can't move the controls!" said Polly. "They're stuck together!"

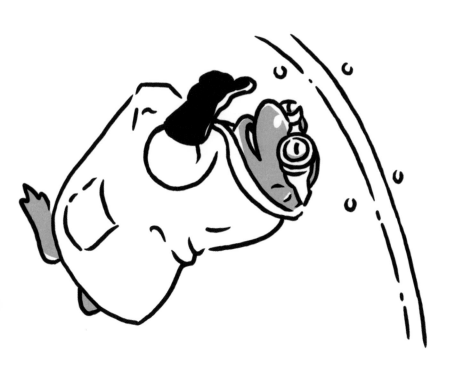

"Ah, magnetism, a most splendid
and powerful force! One of my
favorites," said the hero of science.

"We need to smash it with hammers."

"Oooo!" said Tad.

He and his uncle worked
themselves free.

"Our ship has become a big magnet," said the professor.

"We need to *de*magnetize it. If you hit a magnet hard enough, you make it weaker!"

"You do?" asked Tad.

"Yes," said his uncle. "It's science. You can look it up. But first, Junior Science Heroes . . . grab a hammer and jam into your outer core suits!"

They crawled out of the ship and into the molten metal.

"Oh, and," said their uncle, "zip your suits up tightly. At this depth, the outer core is over . . . **SIX THOUSAND DEGREES!**"

They banged away at the ship.

"How will we know when we're done?" asked Polly.

"When we hear my spoon hit the floor inside," said Tad.

They banged away some more.

Bang! Bang! Listen . . . listen . . .

Bang! Bang! Listen . . . listen . . .

Bang! Bang! Listen . . . *clink.*

"Success!" said the professor.

They went back inside the ship.

"Nothing is sticking to anything anymore," said Polly.

"Outstanding!" said her uncle.

"Junior Science Hero Polly, take Wiggles straight down. Junior Science Hero Tad, strap yourself in as we squirm our way to the . . .CENTER OF THE CENTER OF THE EARTH!"

Chapter 10

TEN THOUSAND DEGREES!

Wiggles swam through the liquid outer core.

"It's been a week," said Polly.

"Shouldn't we be at the inner core?"

CLUNK!

"What was that?" asked Tad.

"That is Wiggles landing on the inner core. We have done it, Science Heroes!"

"Are we going to tunnel inside it?" asked Polly.

"Impossible," said her uncle.

"The inner core is solid iron and nickel. There isn't a ship I could invent that could eat through that."

"Uncle?" asked Tad.

"Yes, Junior Science Hero Nephew?"

"Why are we floating?" asked Tad.

"According to the ship's gravity meter," said Polly, "there is none."

"Correct! There is no gravity at the Earth's core!" said the professor.

"Now cram into your inner core suits. The magnets in the boots will hold us down as we walk on . . . THE VERY SURFACE OF EARTH'S CORE!"

The Science Heroes suited up and

squeezed out the hatch.

"Oh, and," said their uncle, "zip your suits up tightly. The inner core is nearly . . . **TEN THOUSAND DEGREES!"**

They explored the surface of the inner core, but even in their suits, it became too hot.

When they returned to the ship, it was melting.

"Everyone inside!" shouted Albert Hopper.

"Everything is melting!" said Polly.

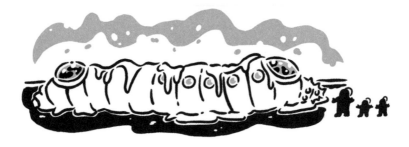

"Take Wiggles up!" ordered her uncle.

"I can't!" said Polly.

"The controls are like rubber!"

"There's only one thing left to do," said Tad.

"I am pressing the A-C-H button again."

"Do NOT!" said his uncle.

Tad's finger inched toward the button.

"I have to press it," he said.

"Don't do it, Tad," said Polly.

Tad's finger touched the button.

"I cannot NOT press it!" shouted Tad.

"You must NOT NOT press it!" ordered his uncle.

"YOU JUST TOLD HIM TO PRESS IT!" cried Polly. "AGAIN!"

Tad pressed the button.

"Sorry," he said.

"What happens now?" asked Polly as their ship melted away.

"Anything, again, I suppose," said the hero of science.

Chapter 11

MOMENTS LATER . . .

Moments later . . .

"Behold! Our newest ship! I call it . . . 'Wiggles,'" said the Science Hero. "We shall be . . . WORMING TO THE CENTER OF THE EARTH!"

"Did we just jump back in time?" Tad whispered to Polly.

"*Yes*," she whispered back.

"So we're back at the beginning of the story?" asked Tad.

"Yes," whispered Polly. "Please don't press that button this time."

Polly's Notes -
Super great trip! (both times) I learned
some fun things.

Layers of the Earth

Crust — outer skin of our planet.
3 to 20 miles thick.
It has 3 kinds of rocks:

- SEDIMENTARY (made under water)
- IGNEOUS (was once magma!)
- METAMORPHIC (changed by pressure from sedimentary or igneous)

Magma — melted rock under the crust.
Can be over 2,000 degrees!
It's called lava when it's above the crust.
                    (which I already knew)
Volcanoes are where pools of magma get
  pushed out to the surface.
                    (knew that, too)

The continents float on <u>tectonic plates</u> made of different kind of rocks. The oceans sit on <u>oceanic plates</u>. (don't call them dishes)
The plates are always moving. When they bump into each other, earthquakes happen.
<u>(not</u> FUN!)

<u>Lithosphere</u> — where the crust meets the mantle. It's always moving, but very, very slowly.

<u>Mantle</u> is below the crust. It's about 1,800 miles thick. It got more solid the deeper we went. It got hotter, too! At the top it's over 1,000 degrees. At the bottom it's 4,000 degrees!!!

<u>Outer core</u> — all mushy and made of mostly melted metals like iron and nickel. And it's SUPER hot! It's also where Earth's <u>magnetic force</u> comes from. (Uncle and Tad got stuck to the ceiling!!! It was pretty funny)

<u>Inner core</u> is solid. It spins around inside the outer core which is all melty. And it's hotter than the sun. Our ship melted, but we got away. You won't believe how.

Uncle Albert- He's a true hero of science! I hope I can be like him someday.
Tad- Don't get me started.

Tad's Notes
(I'd rather draw pictures)